If I were an ...
astronaut

Written by Annabel Blackledge
Illustrated by Jill Saunders

PANGOLIN BOOKS

If I were an astronaut,
I'd wear a silver suit,

a silver helmet,

silver gloves ...

and

great,

big,

bouncy

boots.

If I were an astronaut,
I'd fly off ...

...to the Moon.......

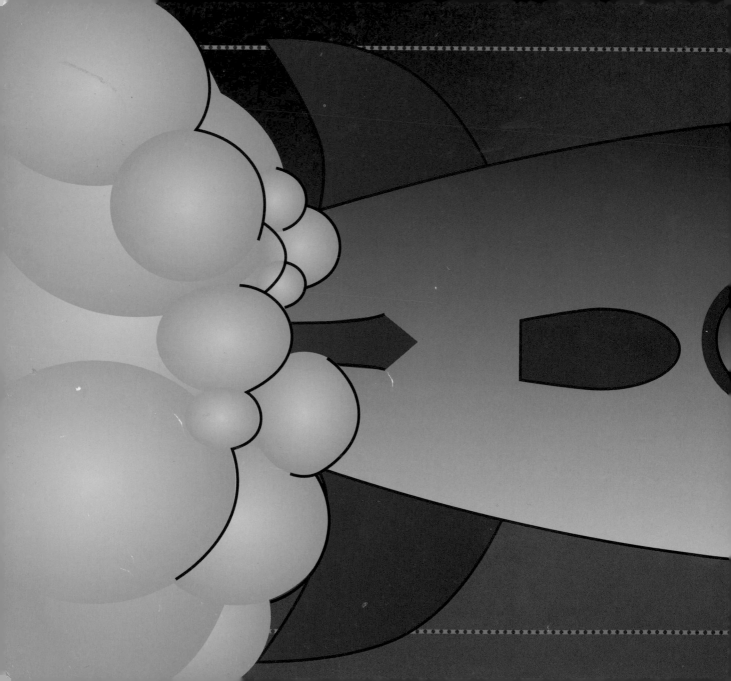

past planets, suns and stars,
and get there very soon.

and look around for any signs of life.

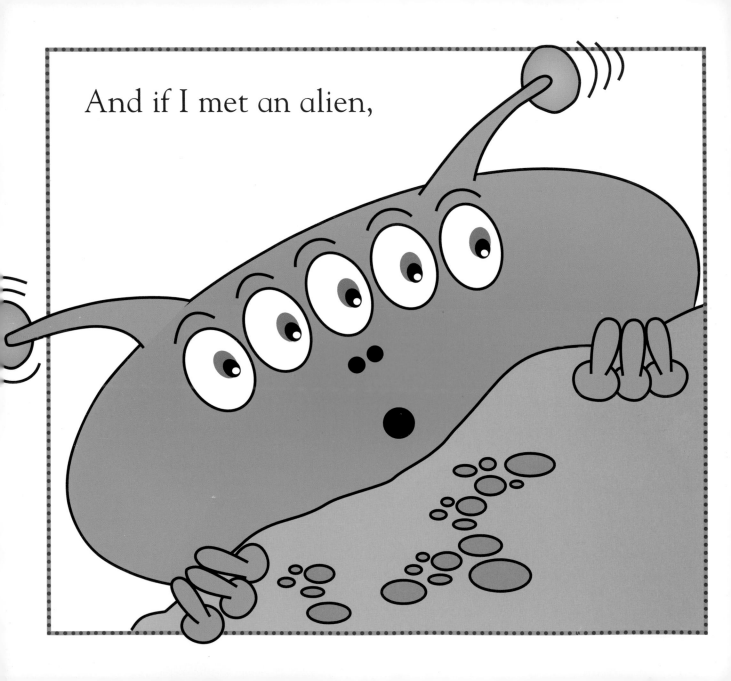

And if I met an alien,

I'd say, "Hello, how nice!"

I'd send a message
back to Earth,

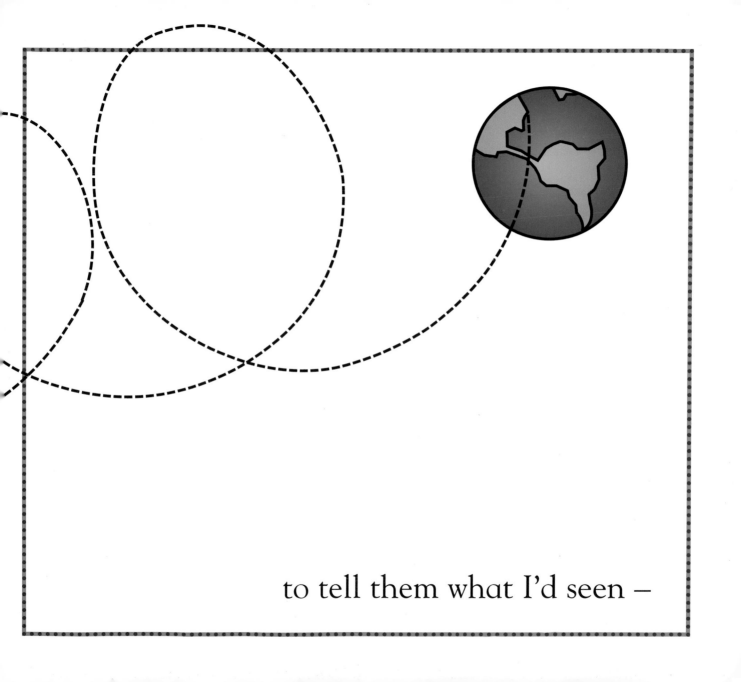

to tell them what I'd seen –

the alien,

the shooting stars,

the suns that **burn** and gleam.

I'd go exploring on the Moon,

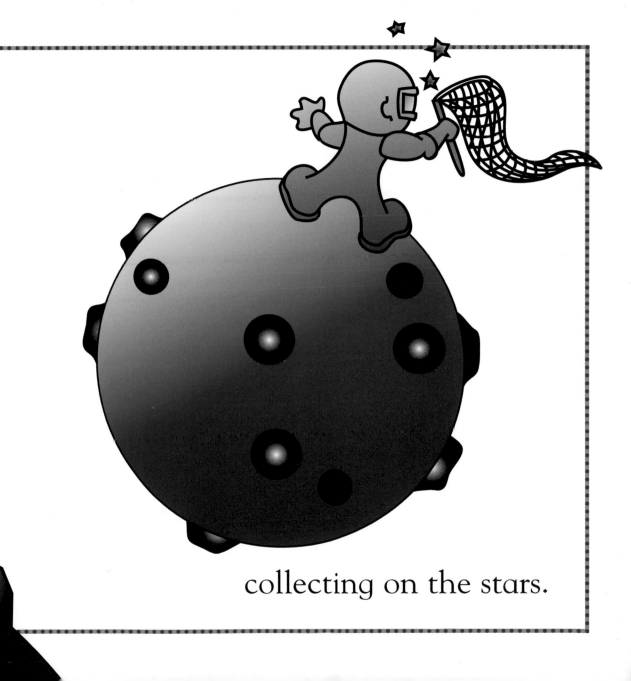

collecting on the stars.

I'd fill my pockets with space dust ...

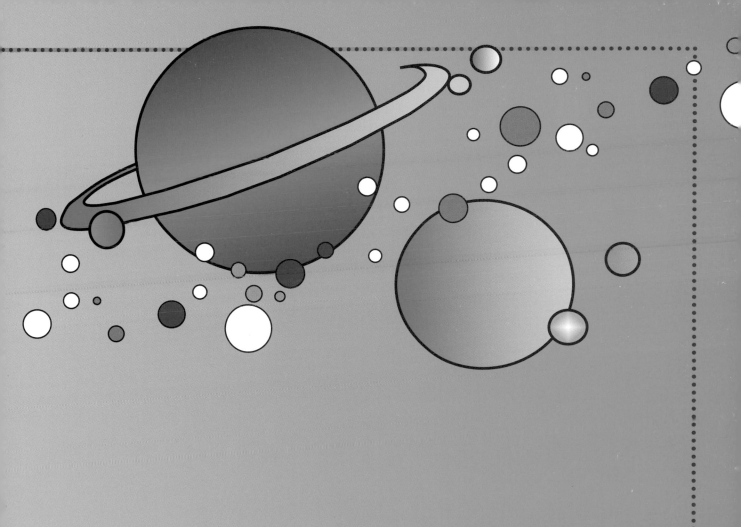

from Jupiter and Mars.

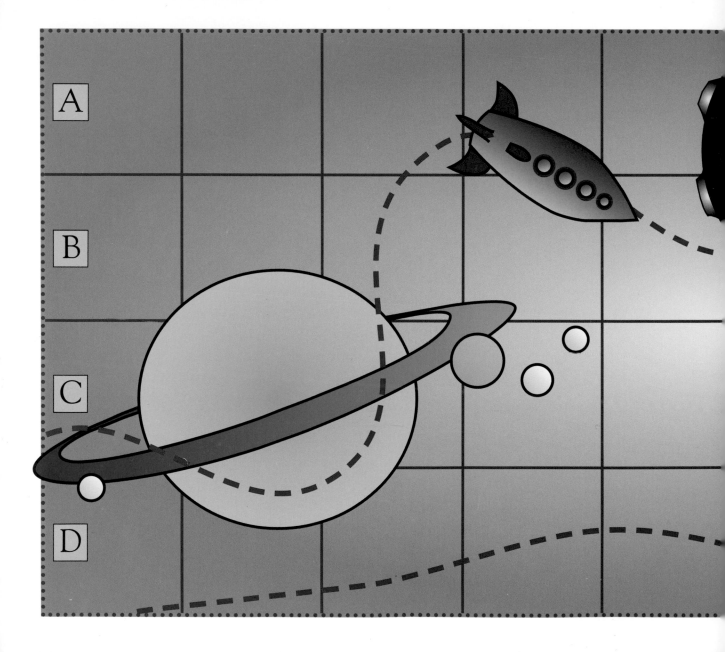

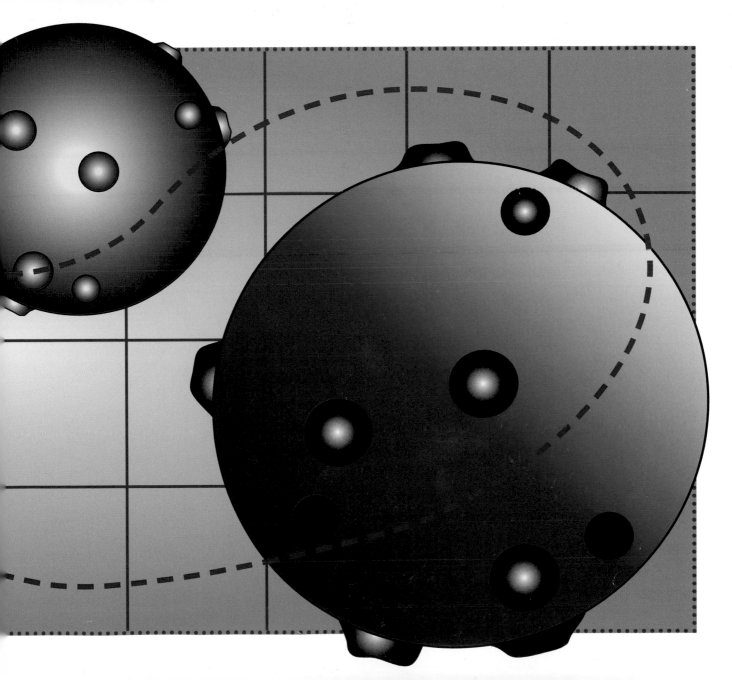

If I were an astronaut, I'd

f l o a t...

and leap

through space.

And then when I was tired out ...

I'd touch down back at base.

First published in the UK in 2004 by:

Pangolin Books
Unit 17, Piccadilly Mill, Lower Street,
Stroud, Gloucestershire, GL5 2HT

Copyright © 2004 Bookwork Ltd

A CIP catalogue for this book is available
from the British Library.

ISBN 1 84493 016 5

Colour reproduction by
Black Cat Graphics Ltd, Bristol, UK
Printed in the UK by Goodman Baylis Ltd